the world's GREATEST underachiever

HankZIPZER

THE COLOSSAL CAMERA CALAMITY

THEO BAKER

WALKER
ENTERTAINMENT

First published in Great Britain 2015 by Walker Entertainment,
an imprint of Walker Books Ltd, 87 Vauxhall Walk, London SE11 5HJ

Based on the television series "Hank Zipzer"
produced by Kindle Entertainment
in association with DHX Media Ltd.
Based on the screenplay *The Colossal Camera Calamity*
Reproductions © 2014 Hank Zipzer Productions Limited

2 4 6 8 10 9 7 5 3 1

Text © 2015 Walker Books Ltd
Cover by Walker Books Ltd

This book has been typeset in OpenDyslexic

Printed and bound in Great Britain by Clays Ltd, St Ives plc

British Library Cataloguing in Publication Data:
a catalogue record for this book is available from the British Library

ISBN 978-1-4063-5973-2

www.walker.co.uk

This book has been set in OpenDyslexic –
a font which has been created
to increase readability for readers
with dyslexia. The font is continually
being updated and improved,
based on input from dyslexic users.

CHAPTER ONE

My dentist is insane. I'm pretty sure all dentists are. If I had to spend all day with my hand in a stranger's mouth, I'd probably lose my mind too. For one thing, he hums "Ring a Ring o' Roses" all the time. Odd, yes, but the crazy part is that he's been humming it ever since I was three. That means he's had the same nursery rhyme worming through his brain for nine years. Nine years! That should tell you quite a lot about him.

There's also his obsession with ducks.

His office is packed with ducks. Paintings and posters of ducks cover the walls, hundreds of duck figurines stand on every available surface – even his surgical mask has a duck's bill. This means that while he's scraping my teeth, what I experience is a duck-man mutant humming "Ring a Ring o' Roses" – or worse, a duck-man lecturing me on proper oral hygiene.

In my dentist's strange and frightening world, I should brush my teeth *three* times every day, and each one should last *fifteen* minutes. Whenever I eat so much as a grain of rice, I'm supposed to dash to the loo and gargle mouthwash, brush my teeth front and back, brush my tongue top and bottom, *scrape* my tongue top and bottom, floss thoroughly, gargle a little more mouthwash, and then when I've finished all that, I should spend another ninety seconds closely inspecting my teeth in the mirror.

It goes without saying that my brushing

technique doesn't live up to his mad standards. I'd say I spend about four minutes a day on it, which isn't bad, considering I have a life. Four minutes of teeth brushing is good enough for most days.

But it wasn't good enough for that day three weeks ago.

That day I had to look perfect.

That morning, I dedicated twenty-one precious minutes to cleaning my teeth. I also spent thirty-seven minutes washing my face, applying moisturizers, cleaning my ears, combing my hair and, for twelve excruciating minutes, I tweezered the seven hairs from my unibrow. (My unibrow hairs are so faint, you need a microscope to see them, by the way.) And, oh yeah, I'd spent an hour the night before ironing my school clothes. And, double oh yeah, I'd slept all night in my bike helmet so my hair would be nice and flat.

What was special about that day?

Was I a contestant in a beauty contest?

Nope.

Was the queen coming to my school, Westbrook Academy, to open the new maintenance closet?

Nope. Have another guess.

Nothing?

OK, I'll tell you. They were taking our school photos.

Wait! Don't leave.

I'm not really that superficial. I'll prove it to you. Come with me to the bookcase in the living room and I'll show you why I needed to look perfect for that school photo.

CHAPTER TWO

This is no ordinary bookcase. This is where my parents display my framed school photos for all the world to see.

Welcome to my shelf of shame.

Last year's photo is probably my best, and that's not saying much. I look very frightened, like I've just seen Miss Adolf dancing. I've seen Miss Adolf dancing, so I know what I'm talking about.

Excuse me while I shudder... *Hhrrhhr.*

So here's the story behind the first photo...

As I sat in the chair, waiting for my
picture to be taken, a spider dropped down
on a thread of silk from the ceiling, and
stopped right in front of my nose. It was
so close I could see its hairy spider legs.
So close I could look into its beady spider
eyes, where I saw its spidery soul. I froze in
fear, my eyes crossed, and … FLASH.

Moving on.

Here's my photo from two years ago.
You'll notice that not much of my actual
face made it into this one. Apart from a
bit of my forehead, it's entirely of the top
of my head. I've always wondered what
the top of my head looks like. Now I know.
You want to know what happened with this
one?

Well, again, I was in the chair, waiting for
my photo, when Frankie told me that my
shoe was untied and I fell for a trick that
was invented a week after they invented
shoelaces. (My guess is they invented

shoelaces in 1684.) Basically, I was stupid for a fraction of a second and ... FLASH. I guess I should be grateful I'm not bald.

And this one here, from three years ago, is everyone's favourite. It's an oldie but a goodie. This one will never go out of style.

No, I'm not picking my nose. Really, I'm not. It just looks that way. I don't pick my nose — at least not when anyone's looking and certainly not when someone is taking my picture. This one was the photographer's fault. He told me to "look smart", so I struck a smart-guy pose.

I put my hand on my chin, like I was thinking about black holes or something, and I guess my index finger decided it would point towards my brain ... by way of my right nostril. With this photo, you get the impression that I'm thinking really hard about bogeys.

I could take you through the rest of the shelf, but it's pointless.

Year in, year out, I take a ridiculous photo. My parents then frame it and put on the shelf. My family laughs at me. Everyone who comes to our flat laughs at me. And every day, as I leave for school, the last thing I see is a shelf of reminders that I can't do anything right.

In eight hundred years, when they're studying what I was like as a kid — because I plan to be the first man to live on Mars and also to hold most major Martian sporting records — they'll find these pictures and the future will laugh at me too.

Then they'll find Emily's perfect pictures, and they'll think she was the really significant one in the Zipzer family. And then they'll form a religion based on Emily and her teachings, and they'll worship the lizard, and the future will be ruined for ever.

I didn't want that happen this year. Do you hear that, ghosts of school photos past?

CHAPTER THREE

Three weeks earlier...

"Hank, stop ogling your photos and come for breakfast," my mum yelled at me.

I took one final look at the top of my head, then flashed my camera-ready smile at the family as I headed over to the table.

"Who is this child?" my mum asked.

"No idea," my dad said. "He must have broken in during the night."

Emily also piped up. "Your photo's not going to look anything like you."

"Good," I said, sitting down.

Mum had gone all out for breakfast: fried eggs, fried bread, beans, bangers and mushrooms. It looked very tasty ... and very *drippy*. This breakfast was a full-body stain waiting to happen. I stared at the heaped plate of food, scanning for just one tasty morsel I could nibble safely.

"Aren't you eating?" Mum asked.

I scooched my chair back about a metre from the table, leaned all the way forward and puckered out my lips, trying to reach just a tiny bite of the egg on my fork with my elastic lips. It was a very awkward position, and all my muscles were shaking, but I couldn't risk dropping anything on my uniform. My lips could feel the heat of the eggs, and then—

Emily kicked my leg.

I dropped the fork, nearly falling backwards to avoid it hitting my leg.

"I was so close." I sighed.

"Just try to eat like a human being and you'll get some egg next time," my dad said.

"I think he was trying out his new pose for this year's photo," Emily said.

"He looked like a monkey." My mum laughed. "Like a baboon."

"Baboons aren't monkeys. They belong to the ape family, Mum," Emily said. "Which reminds me. I've been shortlisted for a summer course at the Institute for Scientific Excellence. My final interview is today."

"That's brilliant," my mum said. "I'll test you on some science thingies. Hmmm." She drummed her fingers. "OK, got a good one for you. What does H_2O stand for?"

Emily dabbed her lips with her napkin. "The covalent bond between hydrogen and oxygen."

"Er ... wrong answer." My mum winked at me. "But here's a hint: it comes out of a tap. This is *fun*!"

Emily just stared at my mum with her beady eyes.

"Emily knows it's water," my dad said. "She was explaining the molecular structure."

"Of course she was," my mum said. "I was ... er ... testing her. Well done, sweetie. Now for a real challenge. What's that table called, you know, that table thingy with all the elements?"

"Oh, come on, Mum," I blurted out, "even I know that one. It's the table of—"

"Eat your breakfast, Hank," Mum said. "And eat it properly, not like a baboon ape. And, Emily, don't roll your eyes at me, young lady. Hank, why aren't you eating? You need your vitamins and ... *claven* bonds."

"You mean covalent bonds," Emily said.

"Don't correct your mother," Mum said.

Emily sighed. "May I be excused?"

"Not until you can ask without rolling your eyes."

As Mum and Emily were engaged in a stare-down that had the potential to last all day, I popped up, ran around the table, gave Mum a kiss, ducked my dad's hand as he tried to ruffle my hair, and shouted, "Bye" as the door to our flat closed behind me.

I'd made it through breakfast still spotless, perfect, and with my gorgeous hair intact. I was flying high!

CHAPTER FOUR

"How do I look?" I asked my best friends, Frankie and Ashley, as we rode down in the lift.

"Weird," Ashley said. "Is that a toupée?"

"Hey, Hank, can I touch it?" Frankie asked.

"Bad idea," Ashley told him. "We don't know what that thing's made of. It could be rat hair."

"Nah," Frankie said. "Looks more like goat hair."

As they bleated and sniggered, I struck

a pose. "You guys don't think my hair looks amazing?"

"It looks fake," Frankie said. "And ruggish."

"Did you say rugged?" I asked.

"He said *ruggish*," Ashley said. "Like it belongs on the floor. Why is it all flat and helmety?"

"Because I slept in my bike helmet."

"I'm no expert on hair," Frankie said, "but I always thought having helmet-hair is, like, a bad thing."

"It is," Ashley said. "Hank, if you wanted to look like Clark Kent, you should have asked me for some hair products."

"I think you should have left the helmet on for the picture," Frankie said.

"Come on, guys," I said as we got out of the lift. "I just need this photo to be perfect."

"Hank, can I tell you something?" Frankie asked. He put his hand on my shoulder and looked at me like he wanted to have a best-mate moment. "You know you're a good-looking guy — I'm not ashamed to say it: Hank, *you are a good-looking guy* — and so you shouldn't worry about how other people see you. Also, your shoelace is untied."

I looked down, and they laughed.

I swung a best-mate punch at Frankie's arm, missed by miles, lost balance, and would have stumbled hair-first into a rubbish bin had Frankie not caught me.

"Easy there, super-rug," he said.

Ashley stopped us. "Hank, you will never make it to the photo without getting messed up. We should go back inside. It's too risky out here."

"It's OK," I said. "We're up after first lesson. I can stay clean till then unless Frankie pulls any more dirty tricks on me."

"Hank," he said, "can I tell you something?"

"No."

"Dude, you know what we've got for first lesson, don't you?"

I shrugged. "Frankie, I don't know what I've got for any of my lessons. I just follow you guys around. What have we got?"

"A problem," Ashley said.

"Why?"

"Because, Hank," Frankie said, "the first class is art."

"Oh, boy."

"And also, dude," Frankie said. "You're flying low." He gestured at the zip of my trousers.

And once again I looked down. But this time, Frankie wasn't kidding. I really was flying low.

CHAPTER FIVE

Most days I can't wait to get to art class.
I can breathe easy in art class. As soon
as I step through that door, it's like I'm no
longer carrying a giant baboon on my back.
I don't have to worry about concentrating
hard on words and numbers or feeling bad
about not being able to concentrate hard on
words and numbers.

My art teacher, Miss Mesmer, is super
cool. Sure, she's a little nutty — not nutty
like my insane dentist, but nutty in a super-
cool way. She has wild frizzy hair, and all

of her clothes are rumpled and stained with cat food and paint. She's usually playing relaxing music with bells and people chanting really slowly when we come in, and before we start painting, she leads us through stretches and breathing exercises, while telling us how gifted and brilliant we are.

She likes me a lot, too, even though I'm not a good painter. And even though I'm not a good painter, I like painting. I like the way the paint smells, and I like mixing all the colours and the way it feels when you paint, and the way you can get lost in stuff like colours.

Miss Mesmer doesn't even make us paint anything that looks real. She just tells us to get messy and paint whatever comes naturally. So I make these giant doodles with different coloured blobs that look like clouds of gas, and while I'm painting I'm not even thinking in words. I'm just concentrating on the way the colours feel and the way the brush feels and the way the painting makes me feel.

And I can totally concentrate the whole lesson. I don't even look up. It must be the freaky bell music Miss Mesmer always plays.

It was major bummer then that we had art class right before the school photo because it meant I couldn't get into the lesson like I usually did. I didn't want to risk messing up my special school-photo outfit. And it was a double-bummer-bonus round when I arrived not to the sound of bell music, but the swoosh of a fencing sword.

Miss Adolf!

"Find your places, pupils," she barked. "Miss Mesmer is out today with emotional fatigue, and I can't blame her now that I see what she has to look at all day."

She slashed her sword at all the paintings

in the classroom, stopping it at one of my paintings of giant gas clouds. "This one here is especially poor. No technique, no content, no recognizable forms.

"Today, pupils, we will be concentrating on the basics. You will make an accurate rendering of the still life I have prepared." She flicked her sword at a pedestal with three grey balls and one grey pyramid on it. "I want you all to concentrate on your shading techniques."

As everyone else continued filing in, I started backing out of the door.

"Hey! Where's Captain Haircut going?" McKelty cried.

Miss Adolf swooped round. "Yes, Henry, where are you off to?"

"To the nurse, Miss."

"Yes, you do seem to have a bad case of helmet hair."

"No, it's cos I'm feeling, uh, emotionally ... I'm feeling emotionally flatulent—"

That got a big chuckle from the class. I like to make people laugh, so for one fraction of a second — as long as it takes to snap a picture — I felt all right and easy. But laughter makes Miss Adolf emotionally *flustered*. She silenced the class with a slash of her sword.

"Even if your are emotionally *fatigued*, Henry, I see no need to visit the school nurse. No emotion whatsoever is required of you during this lesson. Now, start rendering geometric solids."

"Certainly, Miss. I'll just replace the rubbish bag for you first. I noticed the bin was full."

"Lovely, Henry. I think that's a far better use of your time than painting."

I was keen to empty the bin because I'd had an idea. A few nights previously I'd been watching this movie about an out-of-control killer virus. All the doctors in it wore these full-body spacesuits when they were working with the virus in the clean room. I figured I could create my own suit from bin bags to protect my clothes from paint splashes.

The rubbish bin was actually almost totally empty, but what was in there — plenty of paint-splattered rags and old plastic bags of decomposing fruit — looked very bin juicy. So instead of hauling out the rubbish, I just placed a new bag on top and then I got to work on a DIY bio-spacesuit.

I used five garbage bags and a lot of tape, but when I was done, I was covered from head to toe. There was even a bag covering my head and hairdo, complete with a breathing slit and eyeholes.

Now that I was covered up, I could get on with my painting. I'd just put a red circle in the middle of my paper when I felt icy cold breath over my shoulder. I turned around to find Miss Adolf behind me.

"Explain," she said. She'd been patrolling

the art room, telling people to make their spheres more "spherical" and their shading more "shaded".

"Well, Miss, I was trying to capture the inner truth of a sphere."

"No, Henry, I meant your outfit." Miss Adolf looked me up and down while tapping her chin with the handle of her sword.

"Trying to stay clean, so I'll look smart for my school photo, Miss."

"What outrageous vanity," she said. "If you showed as much dedication to your school work, or your shading technique, as you do to your looks, you could be a perfectly average student."

She used the tip of the sword to slice through a piece of Scotch Tape on my suit, and my whole biosuit fell to the floor.

"Now, Henry, get into your standard-issue apron," she said and turned away to tear into the next kid's geometric rendering.

"Hey, Haircut," a voice said. "Catch!"

I turned around just in time to see McSmelty launch a fully loaded paintbrush at me.

Time slowed down. I heard my heart beating. I saw drops of black and red paint flying from the rotating brush as it bore down on my perfect uniform.

Noooooooooo.

And I froze, probably wearing the same expression as in last year's school photo.

But just then, another shape flashed between me and the incoming brush.

Frankie!

In one seamless move, he caught the loaded brush, wrapped it up in his apron and then chucked it across the room to Ashley, who was by the art-class sink. She guided the bundle into the sink and immediately poured water all over it.

Did I mention that I have the best friends in the universe?

Unfortunately, now McKelty knew that I was trying to keep my uniform clean. He knew my fear. And now that he knew, and I knew that he knew, I knew he wasn't going to give up until he got me, totally. But he also knew that I knew that he knew— Hold on, I'm getting a headache in my eye.

McKelty kept trying to get me. Every time Miss Adolf turned her back, he'd hurl a brush at me, or chase after me with a paint tube, or paint his hands and try to pat me on the back. It wasn't difficult to avoid him ... for the time being. But given enough time, I'd let my guard down and then McKelty would be right there, waiting to nail me. Or paint me.

So I decided to take him down first. While he was pretending to contemplate the inner nature of his sphere, I found his lunchbox.

I couldn't believe how neat it was inside. Everything was sealed in its own container. No separate food items touched.

For a minute, I was stumped. There was nothing in there I could use. Then I spotted it, lying nestled between thirty individually wrapped grapes — a can of fizzy blackcurrant.

I gave it no less than 143 vigorous shakes. The next time he was thirsty for blackcurrant, he was in for a big surprise.

CHAPTER SIX

From the pages of Emily Zipzer's field notebook…

9:48 a.m., 8th March

I have excelled since birth. I was only seven months old when I spoke my first word: robust. No one heard me. At two years old, I taught myself simple arithmetic with the toy blocks Hank spent his toddler years drooling over. During my fifth year, I became fascinated with falling objects.

I could often be found tossing a football up and down and observing its flight. Just as I was on the cusp of piecing together my theory of gravity, the mother told me that you are not allowed to use your hands in football. "Kick the ball to your brother," she said.

Even though the mother, Hank and, to a lesser extent, the father have tried to thwart me, I have never stopped in my pursuit of excellence. No matter the obstacle, I have proceeded doggedly because I have always known, deep down, that I am destined for greatness.

Today I take the next step towards that destiny in the final interview for the "Leg-Up Future Achievers" Summer Session at the Institute for Scientific Excellence. And nothing will stand in my way. Not even the mother.

Before leaving for school, I lingered in the shadows of the hall and listened to my parents talk over breakfast. As I had feared, the mother had examined the letter from the institute and learned that parents were supposed to come into school for the interview.

The mother has, on several occasions, got into rows with my teachers over trivial matters. For instance, at my last parents' evening, she told my food-tech teacher that she was using the "wrong" minestrone recipe.

Father is coming with me to the interview today and, although he does not like lying to the mother, he does understand why she can't come. He is no Sir Isaac Newton, but he does have a scientific mind. More importantly, though, he is less prone to emotional and spontaneous outbursts than the mother, although only slightly.

I fear my dad will not be able to keep his presence at the meeting a secret from the mother. She has a special gift. She knows when the Zipzer men are lying.

Just before I began this entry, the father phoned me on my mobile. "I really don't feel comfortable lying to her," he said.

"Just be at school at eleven. Alone," I told him.

Yes, it is wrong to lie. But my lie serves a higher purpose. My excellence at the institute might alter the course of humanity! Besides, the mother never asks for my opinion about the things in my life. For instance, she never asked me if I wanted to be born...

CHAPTER SEVEN

I made it through art with only a very minor, black paint stain on my left pinkie. That was good. No, that was *great*. Not so great was the queue of kids waiting to have their photos taken. It snaked all the way down the hallway.

School corridors are risky. There's kids coming and going. Kids stopping to tie their shoes and becoming tripping hazards – and have you seen how dirty those floors are? Kids carrying messy science and art projects. Kids carrying messy science and art projects with untied shoelaces. Kids are who are just dirty and messy in general and like to touch. Kids who are mean and say, "Why are you looking at me like that?" and push you into the rubbish bin.

I started tapping my foot and fidgeting and clenching my jaw. I needed my picture taken immediately.

By the time we got to front of the line, my foot was all tapped out, and I was hearing this clicking sound in my jaw. But we were there. My hair was neat and flat. My uniform was clean. This year my photo would be perfect. The future was mine.

"You don't mind me cutting in?" asked Mr Love, the school headteacher, stepping in front of me.

"Aw, come on," I muttered.

"Relax, man," Frankie said. "That frown's gonna break the lens."

"Are you guys sure there's no paint on me?" I asked as Mr Love took up position in front of the camera. I guessed I might as well use that extra time to make sure I still looked good.

"You look perfect," Ashley said. "Too perfect. Let me just mess up your hair a bit."

With ninja speed, I blocked her hand. "No one touches the hair, 'kay?"

The flash popped in the camera booth. "Actually," Mr Love said, "you didn't get my best side. Try it again, like this."

FLASH.

"No. My chin was too high. Again."

FLASH.

"I think I blinked," he said.

"I think you winked," the photographer said.

"Either way, take it again. Wait, let me just ... er..." Mr Love took out his pocket mirror. He wet his fingertip and ran it along his eyebrow really, really slowly. This was taking for ever. There was no way I could stay clean and neat much longer.

"This is so unfair," I said way too loud, and I also slammed my back against the lockers way too loud.

"What's that, Mr Zipzer?" Mr Love asked, still looking into his pocket mirror.

"How come you," I said, "get to take as many photos as you want?"

"Because," he said.

"Because why?" the photographer said.

"Because," Mr Love said, putting his mirror away, "I'm the public face of this school."

"But I'm the face of the future," I said, letting my most private thought out into the unforgiving land of public school.

"Yeah," said some kid behind us, "with a haircut from Uranus."

The hallway erupted with laughter. In the space of one hour, my hairdo had become a school-wide joke. It's totally lame that you can't ever try something new in school without everyone noticing, and the way they notice is to make fun of you. Maybe I *was* wrong to try to pass myself as something I wasn't.

Or maybe, I was the only one who was right.

I mean, look at Mr Love. Was he saying, "It doesn't matter, it's only a school photo"? No, he was making the photographer take picture after picture until he got one that was perfect. He clearly knew how important this was for his future. He's the head, the top dog – if he doesn't know what he's doing, who does around here?

Mr Love posed, turning this way and that. He shook his head, unsatisfied, and moved his hands around awkwardly. "I feel like I should be holding something," he said to the photographer.

"Couldn't hurt," the photographer said.

"I have just the thing," Love said, snapping his fingers. "Be back in two."

"Next," the photographer barked.

"Finally," I said. There was a folding metal chair in front of the camera, and there was no natural way to sit on it. "Should I sit back or lean forward, Mr—"

"Name?" the photographer said.

"Henry Zippers — I mean, Henry Zipzer," I said. "But everyone calls me Hank. You'll mark down my real name as Hank, right?"

"Uh-huh."

"Hey, Hank!" Frankie shouted. "Don't forget to smile!" Frankie smiled big and wide, showing off a ridiculous set of goofy fake teeth. I started to laugh, but then I noticed that McKelty was standing next to him.

What was he doing there? Was he planning something?

He'd been much further down the queue before. He seemed deep in conversation with Stu Williams — they were probably talking about hair products — but you could never be too careful with McKelty. I kept an eye on him.

"You ready, son?" the photographer asked.

I turned to face the camera and tried to put McKelty out of my mind. I wasn't going to mess up this year's photo by looking at him.

And then everything started happening so fast. Out of the corner of my eye, I caught a glimpse of blond hair. McKelty wasn't talking to Stu any more. He was pulling something from his lunchbox. A can of fizzy blackcurrant — a can of fizzy blackcurrant that I had turned into a military-grade explosive!

I held my breath as he popped the top. The juice foamed a little, then a little bit more, and then it fizzled out and settled. It was a dud.

I exhaled.

But as McKelty brought the can to his

lips for his first sip, it got a second life and liquid started spraying out everywhere in waves so powerful that McKelty lost control of the can. He yelled as the can spun around wildly, and I saw a spray of purple liquid heading right for me.

Time slowed down again. I could see every drop of dark liquid in the air and hear every popping bubble.

I froze, mouth open in an O, eyes crossed, as the wave of blackcurrant crashed over me.

FLASH.

"Next," the photographer said.

"No!" I said.

"Ha ha," McKelty said.

"Ha ha ha," the hall chanted.

"No!" I said. "Take it again. Take it again!"

"Move it along there, Mr Zipzer," Mr Love said, reappearing in the school hall at that very moment. He was holding a skull from science class. "Now, young man. We've got to wrap this up by three."

I slunk out of the chair, dragged myself over to my mates, and sank down on the floor, my wet head in my sticky hands.

"Forget it, dude," Frankie said. "It's only a photo." He smiled at me with his fake teeth.

"Why's the seat all wet?" Mr Love was saying. "Oh well, I think it's better to stand anyway. More powerful — bolder." He held the skull out in front of him and gazed at it, as though he was lost in deep thoughts. "No, no, no. It's not right. It all feels too ... Hamlet. I want to strike a more historical pose — get across the sense of a great leader. Hamlet was too ... too..."

"Indecisive?" the photographer offered.

"Exactly," Mr Love said. "I'll be right back." He jogged from the photographer's booth, handing me the skull as he passed. I wondered if he knew it was a baboon skull.

"Return this to the science lab."

I was too miserable to move. I'd ruined my school photo again. I could almost hear my future self laughing at me. I could certainly hear McKelty laughing at me. He was so clean he was practically glowing.

I gazed at the baboon skull. Even *it* seemed to be laughing at me. And why not? I was wet and sticky and covered in blackcurrant juice. I stuck my tongue out and licked some from my face. It tasted bitter.

CHAPTER EIGHT

"I guess I'm just a loser again," I said as we walked to maths. The blackcurrant juice had mostly dried, but, boy, was it sticky.

"You're not a loser," Ashley said. "Your photo will look..."

"Rugged? Ruggish?" I said.

"*Unique*," she said.

I sighed.

"Who cares?" Frankie said. "All of our school photos are boring. Yours will stand out."

"Because I'm purple."

"There's always next year," Ashley said.

"Why will next year be any different?" I asked. "Don't you guys get it? This happens every year. Every year I do something stupid, or something stupid happens to me. And it doesn't matter if it only lasts a fraction of a second. It's always the same fraction of a second that my photo is taken. It keeps happening. I guess I've got to just accept that I won't be the first kid to walk on Mars and try to live my sad loser life with dignity."

I looked at all the kids in the corridor. They were so happy and normal. I didn't want to be like them all the time. I didn't even want to be like them for a whole day — just for the fraction of a second. All I wanted was not to do something weird or stupid for the fraction of a second in which my photo was taken. With slumped shoulders, I took another step and fell flat on my face.

An untied shoelace.

"Hey, look, everyone!" McKelty yelled from the other end of the hall. "Hank fell! Ha ha ha." Then he chucked orange peels at me. I didn't even try to block them.

"Come on, dude," Frankie said, crouching down in front of me. "Get up."

"Yeah, let us help you," Ashley said, putting out her hand.

"You need to think positively, Hank," Frankie said.

"Think positively," I exclaimed. "Think positively?!" And then I stopped speaking because I'd seen something that made me smile.

"Wow, you cheer up fast," Ashley said as she helped me up.

"Look!" I pointed. "Look!"

Frankie glanced over at the lost property office. "You lose your keys ... again?"

"No!" I gasped. "Lost property. It's genius. The perfect solution. Don't you see?"

"We see *it*, Hank," Ashley said, shrugging at Frankie. "But why don't you tell us what *you* see?"

"I can find another school uniform, get back in line and have my photo taken again. There's still hope!"

CHAPTER NINE

The jumper was too tight and it was cutting
off the blood flow to my brain. The bottom
of it didn't even reach my belly button, but
I didn't care. Properly sized jumpers were
so last year.

"Work it, baby," Ashley said as I strutted
around the lost property office. "Now,
sashay!"

"How do I do that?" I asked.

"I think you make your lips pouty," she
said.

I put my hand on my hip and puffed out

my lips. "Like this?"

"Ooh-ooh-aah-aah!" said Ashley. She was almost crying with laughter, but Frankie was not impressed.

"Focus, Hank," he said. "You are trying to make your photo better. Is this the look you want to be remembered by?"

"Fashion is my life, Frankie," I said, but he only folded his arms. "OK, I'll focus."

I tried to pull the sweater off, but the stupid thing wouldn't go over my head because it was too tight. I grunted and yelled and hopped up and down and did about twenty other useless things until I ended up crashing into some shelves and falling on my bum.

Then something — a very large ball, I think, or at least something spherical and bouncy — fell off a shelf and knocked me on the head. Three more things then fell off the shelf and hit me too. I'm not sure what they were because I was seeing stars from that spherical object and also blinded by the sweater.

Ashley and Frankie tried to pull the sweater off, but it felt as though my head was about to go with it. I howled until finally the jumper snapped off.

When we'd all recovered, Frankie said, "Dude, this place is a washout. You're not going to find anything in here."

"You're wrong about that," I said, noticing a blue rucksack on the floor beside me. It must have fallen off the shelf. "My old bag!"

"And what about that red one?" Ashley pointed to one between my legs.

"Mine too! And look, there's Old Yellow." My favourite ever bag was sitting beside my other leg. When my grandfather, Papa Pete, had given it to me, he had put a chocolate bar in one of the pockets. I, of course, lost the rucksack the first day I took it to school. I unzipped the small pocket now

54

and, wonder of wonder, the chocolate
was still in there – a little smashed and
flattened, but probably still edible. There
was only one way to find out.

"It's good," I said after the first bite.
"You guys want some?"

"Pass," Ashley said.

"Nah," Frankie said. "Let's leave. There's
nothing in here that will fit you."

"There is one uniform that would fit..." I
said, eyeing Frankie and his jumper and his
shirt and tie.

"Forget it, man. I don't give up my
threads for anyone."

"Come on," said Ashley. "He's your best
friend."

"I've never seen him before in my entire
life," Frankie said.

I took another bite of delicious
chocolate, peanuts, caramel and nougat.
Which made me think, what exactly was
nougat? Was it a type of nut that I didn't

know about? Or maybe it was one of those weird exotic fruits my mum went crazy for, like persimmons. I shook my head to get rid of the thought. Now was not the time to think about persimmons. *Focus, Hank.*

"Can I interest you in a trade, then, Frankie?" I asked, waving the half-eaten chocolate bar at him.

"I don't want an old-rucksack-mystery bar."

"No, but guess what my mum made me for lunch?"

"My favourite pudding?" he asked.

"Your favourite pudding," I said.

"You know, Hank, you've always been my best friend," Frankie said, pulling his jumper over his head.

CHAPTER TEN

**From the pages of Emily Zipzer's field
notebook...**

12:51 p.m., 8th March

I am trying to stay positive, but I fear I am
losing control.

Let me start at the beginning.

Dad arrived punctually at 10:55 a.m. and
met me outside the science classroom,
where all the shortlisted candidates were
to be welcomed by Dr Mehat, who will be

conducting the interviews.

I had half-expected Dad to arrive hand-in-hand with the mother, but he came alone. He was, however, visibly nervous and sweaty, and he was wearing his most unflattering jumper. The black one he's had since his university days and is two sizes two small. The mother hates it. On this point, I have to agree with her. Dad loves it, though. He insists that it's his lucky sweater. Lucky for what?

As we filed into the classroom, Dad attempted several times to change my mind about the mother. "Think how you'd feel if your daughter didn't want you around?" he said.

"The question is meaningless," I replied. "I don't have a daughter."

He tried again. "How would you feel if Katherine didn't want you around?"

Again, the question was without merit. Lizards have limited emotional responses.

Dr Mehat and Mr Love greeted everyone on the shortlist warmly. Mr Love commented on the mother's absence. The father said she was tied up at work. Mr Love seemed to approve. "Probably for the best," he said.

Dr Mehat then spoke in generalities about the institute and the summer programme — information which I was already familiar with from the institute's website. I observed her intently, though, to try and find in her speech, her choice of words, her body language any insight into her character that I could take advantage of in the formal interview. She gave nothing away, so I began to use this time to size up my competition.

There were ten candidates in all, including Molly Phillips. Molly shows no real vigour in her studies and has gravitated to the flaky subject of cold fusion simply to sound smart.

Amit Kahn was also in attendance.

I know little about him or his studies. He is in the year above me. I watched him a moment. He wore small horn-rimmed glasses, which he adjusted frequently, when not biting his nails. His eyes, however, showed a look of calm intelligence. I will have to make an effort to get to know him better.

After a brief observation of the other contestants, I concluded that none of them posed a threat. I watched Mr Love for a while. He was staring intently and at great length and with great interest at a full-size skeleton of a baboon.

After the welcome meeting, we went to wait our turn. I must admit that I became slightly nervous at this time.

Dad noticed and told me to relax. "You don't want to choke when you get to the crease," he said.

I had no idea what he was talking about and told him so.

"I'm talking cricket," he said. "If you're too uptight, you'll be out for a duck. Stay loose and you can hit it for six."

I asked him if this was supposed to be helping.

He said he was trying to "prep me for the big game" and went on to mention several more analogies having to do with cricket. I did not appreciate his comparing scientific excellence with a mindless sporting event. "If anyone needs prepping, it's you," I said.

He was outraged by this. "I interview people for a living!" he said. "There's nothing the doc can throw at me that I can't handle."

I then asked him a few basic questions about the institute and the "Leg-Up Future Achievers" Summer Session. It turned out he knew nothing whatsoever about either.

"We might as well not bother going in," I told him, "if you can't even say what it is you like about the institute."

"She's not going to ask me that question. You're the one applying for the course."

I told him that he was here to show support for my interest in science. To which he replied, "We bought you a lizard, didn't we?"

I dearly wished Katherine was with me. She would have been of more use.

I became even more tense then, and grew more so as the wait dragged on, especially when I heard each applicant exit the interview room to laughter and friendly words from Dr Mehat. Several times I considered asking my dad to leave before the interview.

At 12:29 p.m., one minute exactly before my interview with Dr Mehat was scheduled to begin, my plans started to unravel.

The mother, perhaps sensing an opportunity to ruin my life for ever, chose that moment to call Dad on his mobile. I begged him not to answer it. "Let it go to voicemail. She can tell when you're lying."

He hesitated for a second and then said, "No, I'd better answer it. She might get suspicious otherwise."

My dad is a good man. An honest man. A simple man.

A fool.

He answered the call. "Hi, love, how's it going? ... Emily? No, why would I have heard from her? She's probably at that interview... No, I mean ... I really, really think she wanted to do this on her own... Lying?" he protested, his voice rising an octave. "Why would I lie about this?'

At that moment, Dr Mehat poked her head out of the interview room and called my name.

Oh, gentle reader of the future, have you ever wanted to just disappear into the floor? I did. And so I fell to the floor, and tried to hide under the bench.

Dr Mehat called my name louder.

Dad, meanwhile, was still talking to the mother. "No, love, no one is calling Emily Zipzer." He then made up a ridiculous story about being in a pet shop to pick up some lizard food and some parrot shouting, "Am I a hipster?"

Yes, he actually said that. I wonder if it is possible that I'm adopted.

Dr Mehat overheard this entire confabulation. She looked very confused, so I told her that Dad was an actor. "He's working on a new role. Perhaps you saw him in his latest commercial. For a product claiming to cure athlete's foot." She had not, but she did agree to reschedule our appointment for a later time.

CHAPTER ELEVEN

"It's good to know how easily you can be bought," Ashley said to Frankie as we headed down the hall to our next lesson. "All it takes is a little pudding, huh?"

"Mmm," Frankie said.

"That's all you have to say?"

"Mmm-hmm."

"Hey, look," hollered a kid from the year above. He pointed at Frankie.

The girl with him giggled. "It's the purple pudding monster!" she said.

Frankie was so busy with his cake that

he didn't even hear them.

"In exchange for something sweet,' Ashley said, "you'll wear clothes with blackcurrant stains and let people laugh and point at you?"

Frankie took another tiny little bite of my mum's extra special, chocolate-chocolate sugar treat, so he could savour every last moment of it. "If we do a permanent swap, can I get one of these every day?" he asked me, ignoring Ashley.

My mum's pastries are ridiculously good. When we were really little, Frankie and I would share our lunches. I would give Frankie half of my pastry – the bigger half – and he'd give me half of his strawberry milk. We stopped trading lunches a while back, but every now and then I give him a bit of pastry, when I'm feeling especially nice, or I want something.

"Hey, Hank," Ashley said suddenly. "Isn't that your dad?"

I followed her finger, and my heart travelled up to my throat. The man in the poorly fitted jumper talking into a mobile phone was definitely my dad. But why was he here? Had I done something wrong? And why was he wearing his ridiculous "lucky" jumper?

"He can't see me in these clothes!" I cried, in a white-hot panic.

I spun around and would have darted behind a row of lockers, had I not run sweater-first into Frankie. Our collision made a strange sound – like a bowling ball squelching into a mud pit.

"My pudding!" Frankie said. He began to scrape up the pudding. He even put a bit of it in his mouth.

"Frankie!" Ashley cried. "Think of the germs."

"Three-second rule!" Frankie said. He put another handful in his mouth. "It's still good."

Ashley rolled her eyes. "You are going to get so sick."

Frankie ignored her. He was still trying to pick the pudding up off the floor. "Where's the rest of it?" he asked, panic in his voice.

"On my sweater," I said.

"On *my* sweater," he said, looking up at me. "Now you're wearing my jumper *and* my pudding. You owe me a new jumper and a new pastry."

"Why'd you freak out like that at seeing your dad?" Ashley asked me.

"Dad can't see me in this uniform. It's the third one I've ruined this term."

"And that one isn't even yours," Frankie grumbled.

I surveyed the damage to my new sweater (or if you like, Frankie's old sweater). It was toast. And so were my tie and my collar. I was a chocolate-y mess. A fraction of a second had yet again ruined me for ever.

Ten seconds ago, the plan had been perfect. It didn't matter that I hadn't quite worked out how I was going to convince the photographer to take my photo again. I had a rough idea involving my identical twin, and I was confident I could convince him. The important thing was that I had a clean uniform. And then my dad had turned up to prowl the school halls and ruined everything!

He must have been there because of Emily's science thingy. They were acting all buddy-buddy at breakfast. I bet she secretly asked him to come for the interview and not tell Mum. I bet she took a perfect picture today too. And I bet this summer she'll be heading towards scientific excellence – probably preparing to be the first kid on Mars – while I hang around at home in Frankie's stained jumper...

"... still don't get it," Ashley was saying. "Everyone's uniform looks the same. How would he know it was Frankie's?"

I snapped back to the present. "Oh, I guess he wouldn't. You're pretty smart, Ashley."

"Well, thank you!"

I looked Ashley up and down, and put my hand on my chin. "And you look very smart today, I must say. You always look smart. But you look especially smart today. New shampoo?"

"This is getting weird."

"Yes, you really do look smart in that jumper and that tie and that—"

"Don't *even* think about it. I'm not giving you my uniform."

"I just need the top half. You can keep the skirt."

"Uh, I think I'm keeping all of it. Hello? Height difference."

"Oh yeah," I said, my eyes level with her chin. "You're smart, Ashley. You know that?"

"Not going to happen, Hank. You'll just have to stay in Frankie's pudding-coated jumper or go back to lost property and get that tiny jumper."

"You know, super-tight sweaters are in," Frankie said.

"They were actually in ... last year," I said.

"Really?"

"No." I sighed. "What am I going to do? Even if I can convince the photographer to snap me again, I won't have a clean jumper. And right now I look like the Pudding Monster."

Frankie patted my shoulder. "Face it, Hank. This perfect-photo thing is just not happening this year, dude. You're going to have to deal with having a unique picture." He crossed his eyes to punctuate his point.

I groaned.

Right then, Karen, the prettiest girl in school and who I've had a hopeless crush on for years now, came walking by. She was with Jack James, a big square-jawed athlete with steely blue eyes and never a hair out of

place. Bet he never ruins his school photos —
he probably looks brilliant in all of them.

"Hey, nice haircut!" Karen called out and
giggled.

I just stood there, hoping the floor would
open and swallow me up.

"Looks like your mate with the haircut
needs a bib," Jack said to Karen, who
giggled some more. Then she stopped
giggling and started blushing when he put
his arm around her.

That was when I decided enough was
enough. This year I was going to own my
school photo. It was time for the Ziper man!

"I am not giving up," I said resolutely.
"This year is my year cos I'm going to run
home and get my spare uniform."

"There's no time," Ashley said. "It's
already twenty to two. Classes start again
in ten minutes."

"There's plenty of time," I said. And I
started off towards the exit.

"But the photographer's leaving at three!" Ashley called after me. "Hank! Wait! What will I tell Miss Adolf?"

"I had a fashion emergency!"

I broke into a run once I had safely passed by Mr Love's office. He seemed to be playing dress-up in there. He was standing in front of the mirror with one hand tucked in his vest and a three-cornered hat on his head.

He reminded me of a crazy man I met in the park last summer. He'd had his hand in his vest and a hat like that too. He'd called himself Napoleon.

I should mention that Mr Love had also been having a full-on conversation with his image in the mirror.

"Hey!" Frankie yelled. "Come back with my pudding!"

CHAPTER TWELVE

THE INSTITUTE FOR SCIENTIFIC
EXCELLENCE OFFICIAL EVALUATION
FORM FOR "LEG-UP FUTURE
ACHIEVERS" SUMMER SESSION,
WESTBROOK ACADEMY

Evaluator: Dr Meera Mehat, PhD, MD
Evaluee: Emily Zipzer

Evaluator's Notes:
*Having reviewed Miss Emily Zipzer's sterling
written application, I was very much looking*

forward to chatting with this promising young lady. I considered her the strongest candidate. However, I was unable to meet with Miss Zipzer at the appointed time, as her father, Stan Zipzer, was engaged in a mobile phone call. (Minus 5 points.)

What follows is a full transcript of my interview with Emily Zipzer and her father.

DR MEHAT: Shall we continue?

STAN ZIPZER: You bet. Fire away, doc! Oh, boy. I mean, Dr Mehat... Er, I mean, Your Grace. Or would you prefer Your Honour? Herr Doktor? Sorry, I sometimes slip into German. Those things happen when you're fluent in half a dozen languages.

DR MEHAT: Meera will be fine.

STAN ZIPZER: Brilliant! Call me Stan. It's nice dropping formalities, eh? I think you and me, *Meera, get* each other. You might even say we have a real convalescent bond.

NOTE: It is this evaluator's opinion that Mr Zipzer was referring to a "covalent" bond.

EMILY ZIPZER: Take a breath, Dad.

STAN ZIPZER: Of course I'm breathing, Em. I would keel over if I wasn't, right, Meera, scientifically speaking, of course, Your Grace? Is there a window or something we can open in here? Bit stuffy, no? Bit hot too. Anyone else hot, or is it just me?

DR MEHAT: I'm adequately comfortable.

STAN ZIPZER: Think I'll take off this sweater...

EMILY ZIPZER: I'm sorry about my father, Dr Mehat. He's nervous cos he ... just got a call from the hospital. About ... my mum.

DR MEHAT: Oh, my.

EMILY ZIPZER: She runs a small
business — a deli — and she lost
most of her arm, from below the
mid-humerus, in the salami-mincing
machine.

STAN ZIPZER: Yes, we couldn't believe
it when that happened.

EMILY ZIPZER: That's why it's so
crucial that I'm accepted into
your esteemed "Leg-Up Future
Achievers" summer course. I want
to give Mummy something to smile
about again. I'm sorry. I don't mean
to cry. It's just all … so terrible…

DR MEHAT: I understand. Do you feel
up to a few questions?

EMILY ZIPZER: I think so, Meera.

CHAPTER THIRTEEN

As I ran, I tried to do the maths. I could run from the flat to school in twelve minutes, easy, which meant that once I got home, I'd have twenty minutes to get dressed, redo my hair and floss my teeth, then another twelve to fifteen minutes to run back. If I added in a couple minutes for exhaustion, I'd get back to school at approximately... Well, I'd get back to school with a little time to spare. It's hard to add minutes and hours together. Try it.

I was on track to make it home in eleven

minutes — a new world record, although not a Martian one. As I rounded the corner of my street, I got the Zipzer sense that all was not right in the world. I slowed down. I checked my shoelaces. I checked my fly. All good there. But that was the only good thing about these trousers, because these were not my trousers.

And that meant the keys in my pocket were not my keys. That was not my gorgeous face smiling up at me from my school ID card.

I really started to dislike Frankie's face at that particular moment.

Exhausted and frustrated, I sank down onto the pavement. A woman walked by and dropped a quid on the ground in front of me. I bought a bottle of water from the corner shop with it and a chocolate bar with a quid from Frankie's wallet. Now I owed Frankie one jumper, one pound and one pudding from Mum's deli.

Of course — the deli!

I could find Papa Pete and get the spare keys off him.

The deli was a six-minute sprint from the flat. I still had time. I still had a little life in me.

I ran through puddles. I ran through traffic. I ran like the fastest man on Mars. I ran until my side was burning and I nearly threw up the chocolate bar. I only stopped once, to check through a bin, in case some kid had decided to chuck his uniform in it on his way home from school yesterday.

When I got to the deli, I saw Papa Pete through the window. He was clearing tables. Mum was nowhere to be seen. That was good. Papa Pete would be cool about the ruined school photo, the trashed uniform and the lost keys. My mum? Not so much.

I got down low and pressed my hands and face up against the window, trying to send a telepathic message for him to look over at me. Even though I couldn't see Mum, I decided it was too risky to go inside without knowing exactly where she was. I didn't want her to appear at the wrong moment.

A man with a very obvious toupée looked at me. Since my hair was all messed up, and my face was dirty, and my hands, shirt and tie were smeared with chocolate, the guy must have thought I was Oliver Twist, begging for scraps. He shook me off with a snooty sniff and flipped open his newspaper.

I smushed myself up against the glass and tapped as loudly as I dared until I finally got Papa Pete's attention. Then I gestured for him to come outside. But Papa Pete gestured for me to come inside. I gestured for him to come outside. Like my regular vocabulary, my gesture vocabulary is not very extensive. Then a woman with a tray stepped between him and me.

Mum!

I dropped to my knees before she saw me. She started talking to Papa Pete, so I pressed my ear against the glass. I could al*most* hear what they were saying.

"What are moo doing?" I heard her ask Papa Pete, though I doubted she said "moo."

I could not let Mum know I was here. I waved frantically at Papa Pete in a gesture that had to mean "Don't tell her I'm here."

Papa Pete froze, mid wave. Then he flexed his muscles. "Wiping down tables can be flossing," I sort of heard him say. "Got a cramp in my farm."

"Really?" Mum said, "because it looked like you were waving to Shank through the clindow."

I looked about to determine who this Shank character was, and what in the world a "clindow" was and found myself staring right into Mum's eyes.

I waved hello!

She crooked her index finger at me, gesturing "come here." That is the worst gesture in the world.

CHAPTER FOURTEEN

"So let me get this straight, Hank," my mum was saying. "You ruined two uniforms in one day. And now you want to ruin a third?"

"The second one wasn't my fault. It was—"

"Is that my pastry on your sweater?"

"Like I was saying, Mum, it's Frankie's sweater. Just listen to me for one sec—"

She reached down and plucked off a flake, and ate it. "It is my pastry! Why is—?"

"It's long story and I don't have time to go into it now."

Just then, the man with the toupée set down his newspaper with a loud "harumph". Then he put on his coat, muttering to himself, and marched over to us. His silver moustache was twitching in anger.

"Madam," he said, "I cannot abide you letting filthy street rats into the dining room. It is simply unsanitary. Until your commitment to hygienic standards is vastly improved, I shan't be returning."

"This street kid, for your information" — Mum flared her nostrils — "is my son." She patted my greasy, sticky hair.

"Then I suggest you bathe him at once. The odour is most unpleasant. Good day."

While I watched Lord Hairpiece leave, my mum was rubbing her fingers together, trying to rub off the gunk from my hair. "What product is this? Is it my Parisian gel?"

"No, Mum. And stop touching my hair,

OK?" I ducked back out of her reach. I was feeling grumpy. It had not been the best day.

"Listen, sweetie," Mum said gently, "it's only a photo. No use getting yourself worked up over something so silly."

"Yes, Hank," Papa Pete said. "We love you no matter what your school photo looks like. We love the real Hank, even the dirty and smelly Hank, not some picture."

I slid out of both of their embraces and sighed loudly. "It's not some silly photo. Why does everyone keep saying that? This is important!"

Mum and Papa Pete exchanged a very long look.

"I'm sorry, love," Mum said, "but your uniform's still in the laundry basket. I was going to wash it tonight."

"Is it covered in chocolate?"

"No, but—"

"Good enough! Just give me the keys so I can get in the flat."

"Hank." Mum sighed. "I don't have time to look for them right now. My keys are — I don't know. Just get Dad to open up for you."

"Can't. Dad's at school."

"Oh, is he now?" She was trying to act tough, but, man, I thought she might cry then and there. Her whole face had drooped. I'd never seen my mum so sad. "Was he there for Emily's science thingy?"

"Dunno. Maybe. I didn't really see him. It might have just been some other guy."

"Was this guy called Stan Zipzer? Did he also answer to the name of Dad?"

"Yeah." I gave her sticky hug. "Maybe. Sorry, Mum."

"Right. Your father and I are going to have words, Hank. Serious words. Pop, can you mind the shop? I'm going out too."

Once she'd left for the backroom, Papa Pete said to me, "Tonight, Hankie, my boy, I think you might see your father cry."

CHAPTER FIFTEEN

Evaluator's interview with Emily Zipzer and her father (cont'd)

> EMILY ZIPZER: One topic I have made
> a study of over the last several
> months is filial cannibalism. It is
> a fascinating subject — one which
> I would love to continue studying
> over the summer at the "Leg-Up"
> programme. Are you familiar with
> filial cannibalism, Dr Mehat?
> DR MEHAT: Not intimately, but I

believe it is a rare phenomenon
where the parent selectively eats
their young.

EMILY ZIPZER: Oh, it's much more
widespread than you'd think. It
occurs across the entire animal
kingdom. Even in primates.

STAN ZIPZER: Such as baboon apes?

EMILY ZIPZER: Yet surprisingly, the
practice is, from my knowledge,
not present in reptiles. I'd like
to investigate why this is. I have
a great deal of respect and
admiration for lizards, and consider
them to be on an equal footing
with mammals.

*Whereupon the door to the interview room
burst open, and ROSA ZIPZER entered.*

STAN ZIPZER: Oh, boy.

ROSA ZIPZER: Hello, Stan, Emily. And
hello, Your Excellency. I'm Mrs
Zipzer. Sorry I'm late.

DR MEHAT: Call me Meera, please. And that's quite all right. Won't you sit down?

ROSA ZIPZER: Thank you.

DR MEHAT: I must say, Mrs Zipzer, you really are looking well. It's wonderful you were able to get away from the hospital to support your daughter.

ROSA ZIPZER: Hospital?

EMILY ZIPZER: Actually, Meera, she was at the prostheses lab, getting her new arm fitted.

ROSA ZIPZER: What are you talking—?

STAN ZIPZER stepped on ROSA ZIPZER's foot.

STAN ZIPZER: These new artificial arms are amazing. They look so real. Don't they, love? Sometimes when we're holding hands over our tea I even forget it's a prosthetic — that's how lifelike it is.

ROSA ZIPZER: Yes, modern technology. Incredible what they can do when you ... *lose an arm*.

DR MEHAT: Simply amazing. May I examine it? Simply for curiosity's sake. This won't be a part of the official evaluation.

STAN ZIPZER: Anything for science.

DR MEHAT: Extraordinary. It looks just like real skin. Wonderful elasticity. Is this made of a polyethylene compound perhaps?

ROSA ZIPZER: Nothing but.

DR MEHAT: May I pinch it, to test its tensile strength?

STAN ZIPZER: Go right ahead, Meera. You don't mind do you, love?

EMILY ZIPZER: She doesn't mind.

CHAPTER SIXTEEN

My life can sometimes seem like a never-ending crisis. It certainly feels that way.

But this wasn't a crisis. This was more like a mission. And missions are fun. I am good at missions. They focus my brain, so that I don't worry about not reading well and I stop thinking about forgetful I am.

Right then I was no longer a forgetful, underachieving kid with helmet hair but a man on a mission. I was a hero! *Yes!* I could do this.

As I hurtled back to the flat with Mum's

keys, I felt like I had a chance. This year was going to be my year. Photographic perfection was within my grasp!

That enthusiasm lasted 3.4 seconds after I entered the flat. I had dashed to the laundry basket, ripped off the lid, flung clothes everywhere in a storm of dirty laundry, and there it was, lying right at the bottom.

My uniform.

My heart sank when I pulled it out, though. I'd let a pen bleed to death all over the shirt collar. At that moment I wanted to be anywhere else but here.

I wanted to disappear into the floor, tunnel through the planet and re-emerge somewhere in Chile with a new name, a new haircut, and a fresh start. As I couldn't do that, I sort of crumpled to the floor instead. While I rubbed my eyebrows into the carpet, I scolded yesterday's Hank for screwing up my life so royally.

There was no time to wallow. I only had forty-ish minutes until the photographer packed up for the day. I had to be sitting in his chair, looking like a million dollars, before he did.

I sprang to my feet and clapped my hands. Time to get heroic.

First thought: stains come out in the wash.

Solution: wash the shirt!

I ran to the kitchen sink and scrubbed the collar. I scrubbed like Cinderella. I scrubbed until I thought my hand would fall off. I scrubbed under the hottest water the tap would pump out. Then I scrubbed under the coldest water, just in case that helped. I froze my scalded hand but did hardly any damage to that stinking stain.

All my hollering and banging around had attracted Katherine the lizard. She was peering at me from between two boxes of cereal, watching me like I was a fly she was hunting. She flicked her tongue out, which

I took as a sign she was ready to help — or maybe she just wanted to eat me.

"What do you think?" I asked her, holding up the shirt. "Can I get away with this?"

Her tongue disappeared.

"No, I didn't think so either," I said and then sighed. "How can I get this out?"

Katherine's tongue appeared again, to lick her eyeball.

"That's just what Emily would say."

I looked at the shirt again. I needed soap.

The kitchen dispenser was empty, so I dashed to the bathroom. I knocked almost everything off the sink as I lunged for the liquid soap. After squirting half of the bottle on the stain, I really let my shirt have it. Still no luck, though my hands now smelled like nectarines.

I was starting to feel panicky. My legs had got wobbly, so I looked around for a soft spot to collapse onto.

Then I saw it. Not a soft spot but a

solution to the problem of my stained shirt. Emily's electric toothbrush. I must have knocked it off the sink earlier. That's what I needed: more muscle.

I squirted the rest of the liquid soap all over Emily's dentist-recommended hypersonic brush. While the tap water was warming up, I looked at myself in the mirror. *You can do this.*

Then I saw something green and scaly reflected in the mirror. Katherine had followed me and was now sitting on the bathtub, watching me. No time to worry about that now.

I took a deep breath, plunged the brush into the steaming hot water and pressed the little blue "start" button. That brush was so super-charged that it sprayed soap and scalding water all over the place.

It didn't get the stain out either.

"Talk to me, Kathy, huh? I'm running out of ideas here!"

The lizard seemed to breathe.

"You're right. A toothbrush only works with toothpaste."

I pulled the cap off Emily's dentist-recommended toothpaste and squeezed some out. I'd never used her special paste before, and it came out all thick and blue... The exact same colour as my shirt!

Idea number two: I opened the cupboard above the sink and got out one of Mum's make-up brushes. After applying some of Emily's gross paste to it, I painted over the black ink stains.

When I was done, I held the shirt up to the mirror. It looked all right, not perfect, but good enough. At worst, people would think my shirt had a minor factory defect.

But Katherine seemed to disapprove. She was licking her eyeball again.

"If you tell *anyone* about this," I said to her, "I'm taking you back to the pet shop."

Katherine licked her other eyeball. That

meant she agreed — in lizard speak, of course.

Phase three: fresh jumper.

Next crisis: the jumper in the laundry was creased. But I was in hero mode and knew what to do immediately.

My face was all damp, because I'd steamed up the bathroom with all the hot water. Steam would get the crease out.

I ran back to the bathroom, turned on the hot taps in the sink and the shower. Then I put the jumper on the floor and rolled all over it like a human iron. Not wanting to be broiled alive and become dinner, Katherine had scurried away.

I got the crease out in no time, plus my hair was nice and damp for a ninety-second restyle, which is seventy seconds longer than most days.

I buttoned up the shirt, jumped into my jumper, tied my tie, and flashed one last look at myself in the mirror by the doorway.

Everything looked good, everything except...

"Noooo!" I cried and collapsed once again to the floor.

There was a huge, yellow mustard stain, the size of a potato crisp and the shape of a grizzly bear, right smack dab in the middle of the knot of my tie.

I had no idea how *that* stain had got there. I wanted the ground to swallow me up, but since sinking through this floor would only take me to old Miss Delillo's smelly apartment for bitter tea and a concrete scone, I dragged myself over to the sofa and lay down there instead. At least I'd be comfortable in my misery.

From there I had an excellent, unobstructed view of the bookcase, and my shelf of shame.

"Well, boys," I said to the funhouse gallery. "Looks like you'll be getting another weirdo friend soon."

I stared at the empty space where this year's photo would go and imagined how it would look. My mouth would be open in a big, stupid O. My eyes would probably be bugging out of my head — unless they were mostly closed against the blackcurrant wave. With *my* luck, one eye would probably be open and the other would be half closed. And, oh yeah, I'd be covered in a mysterious purple liquid.

I saw the photo, clear as day in its new spot, and it was hideous and ridiculous. It would take twenty minutes to explain why I looked so ridiculous in that photo, and people usually don't want to wait twenty minutes just to learn why something that makes them laugh isn't actually funny.

I'd worked so hard. I'd run into setbacks, nearly disastrous setbacks, but I'd overcome them. Except for the stain, I didn't look half bad. I still had a chance to make it back to school in time, but what was the point?

Psst! Over here!

"Huh?" I said.

I'm looking at you. Over here.

The top of my head was talking to me! And looking at me, too!

"You look pretty good," I said to the face.

I know I do. But no one else does. Want to look like a loser the rest of your life?

"Not really."

Then get off the sofa, a new picture said, the one who had been startled by the spider.

"I can't," I said.

Don't be afraid, Startled Hank said. *I wasn't really afraid, and neither are you.*

"Thanks and everything, guys," I said, "but did anyone notice the stain?"

Ahem, ah, may I make an observation? Smart-Guy-Pose Hank asked.

I sighed. "Go ahead, Dr Bogey."

Very amusing, but you're forgetting Emily's got a spare tie.

"You're right!" I cried and sprang to my feet.

Now go and be bold. You have twenty-three minutes. You must complete your mission. The future depends on you! said the three Photo Hanks together.

Then, as I was running to Emily's room, Em's photo from last year came to life. "Long live the lizard!" it hissed and shot poison from its forked tongue.

Never! The future will belong to warm-blooded mammals!

I grabbed her tie, replaced it with my stained one, and went warp speed to the door to meet my date with destiny!

CHAPTER SEVENTEEN

I ran like the fastest man in the known
universe. I ran like my hair was on fire.
Nothing could stop me, not even a mini-
downpour. As soon as I felt the first drop of
rain on my arm, I saw an umbrella in a bin
up the street, and without breaking stride,
I grabbed it, popped it open, and kept on
going.

Everything was going right. I saw
everything before it happened — couriers,
guys throwing rubbish bags, cars splashing
in puddles. I saw it all in slow motion, and

without thinking about it, I dodged, pivoted or deflected without losing a step of my momentum. And the whole time I ran I made up a perfect airtight story about my fraternal twin to convince the photographer to take my picture again. It was just unbelievable enough to be true.

I made the dash in a record-shattering six minutes — I saw nothing but green traffic lights — and upon jogging through the school doors, I tossed my umbrella to Miss Berkson, the school administrator, and said, "Here's something nice for ya, Berky."

I made it to the back of the queue for photos at 2:47 on the dot. There were four kids ahead of me. If it took each kid one minute for his picture, then I was home free. I'd have my picture taken with a whopping six to eleven minutes to spare. I could use that extra six to eleven minutes to practise my arithmetic.

I rehearsed my fraternal twin story while

the kids ahead of me got their pictures taken.

By the time it got to my turn, my story would be perfect, and the delivery would be a work of art. I would start with nonchalance, then transition smoothly into mild surprise, and then outrage if needed. And if the photographer was still resisting, I knew I could work up some tears. And if tears didn't warm his heart, I always had that fiver in Frankie's wallet.

Finally the last kid was done. I took a deep breath. This was going to work. There was no McKelty and his can of fizzy drink to mess it up.

I am Hank Zipzer, I rehearsed to myself. *Henry Zipzer's fraternal twin... Perhaps I look familiar?*

I took a step forward. And then I heard footsteps approaching behind me. They sounded like a knight in armour. *That is crazy,* I thought. But then something grabbed my arm. A metal hand!

I spun around and found myself looking up at a knight in full plate armour, with a shield, and a sword and a visor and everything.

From behind the visor, a booming voice echoed, "You've already taken your photo, Zipzer. Stop wasting the photographer's time."

"But it'll just take a second, a fraction of a second. Please?"

"Be silent!" the knight boomed.

CHAPTER EIGHTEEN

Evaluator's interview with Emily Zipzer and her father (cont'd)

DR MEHAT: ... which leads me to my
   final question. We consider family
   support to be a vital ingredient for
   success at the institute. Mr and Mrs
   Zipzer, how would you describe the
   Zipzer family and home life?
STAN ZIPZER: Loving, warm, *scientific*.
   Has Emily told you we bought her a
   lizard?

DR MEHAT: At length.

ROSA ZIPZER: And don't forget, Stan, we like to do things together as a family. We know it's not nice if we leave someone out. Because we don't hurt the ones we love.

STAN ZIPZER: Although sometimes people get hurt by accident. You know, through bad luck. Strange things happen in this *wondrous* universe of ours, and no one's really to blame. People get hurt accidentally all the time. I'm very interested in accidents... Perhaps Emily could study them at the institute.

DR MEHAT: If she's accepted, of course.

STAN ZIPZER: Of course, Meera.

ROSA ZIPZER: *Accidentally?!* You mean like *accidentally* losing my arm in a salami-mincing machine?

EMILY ZIPZER: Just the bottom half,
Mum. Below the mid-humerus.

STAN ZIPZER: Don't get upset, love,
you'll damage your stitches. And
you'll need both arms to hold the
flowers I'm going to buy you... I
mean, the ones I've already bought
you.

ROSA ZIPZER: Oh, let go of me. I don't
want to hold your hand, Stan. You
baboon ape! Dr Mehat knows I don't
have a prosthetic arm.

EMILY ZIPZER: I'm coming to the same
conclusion. My parents have been
lying to me. Dr Mehat, do you
see how dysfunctional my home
life is? That's why I need to be
accepted at the institute. I need to
be somewhere where my scientific
gifts are appreciated.

STAN ZIPZER: We bought you that
freaky lizard!

ROSA ZIPZER: How could you both lie to me?!

STAN ZIPZER: Meera, I mean, Dr Mehat, Your Grace, would you mind ... er ... can we redo this interview?

DR MEHAT: No.

ROSA ZIPZER: I suppose you'd leave me out of that one too?

STAN ZIPZER: Rosa, love, Emily just ... we ... just ... I ... just ... thought it would be better if the two of us ... if me and Em. Science isn't your thing, you know.

ROSA ZIPZER: So what?

EMILY ZIPZER: I didn't want you to make a scene, like you did at parents' evening with my food-tech teacher.

ROSA ZIPZER: She was trying to tell me how to make minestrone! Me? Minestrone! I could make minestrone with baboon meat and

it'd still be better than your silly
teacher's recipe.

EMILY ZIPZER: I tried to avoid this
happening, and by trying to avoid
it, it happened. This is quite ironic.

ROSA ZIPZER: Tonight I think I'll try
out a new recipe with lizard meat.

EMILY ZIPZER: No, Mummy, please!
Don't hurt her!

DR MEHAT: Fascinating. The familial
behaviour is fascinating...

CHAPTER NINETEEN

The knight flipped up his visor. It was Mr Love.

"Ah, it's Prince John," the photographer said.

"No, no, no," Mr Love said. "Maybe if you'd studied in school, you'd know that it was Richard the Lionheart who fought in the Crusades."

"You were in the Crusades?" the photographer asked.

"Yes, see here. The red cross on my shield, the red cross on the hilt of my sword. Was Richard left-handed or right-handed? I don't want to hold my sword in the wrong hand."

"Come on, Mr Love," I said. "I just need one second to take my photo. The last one wasn't actually me. Some kid was pretending to be my fraternal twin—"

"No deal, Mr Zipzer. The photographer and I will need this remaining time to get my picture just right. Now" — he tried to unsheathe his sword — "get back to class."

But I wasn't going anywhere, and I was so frustrated that I tore a piece of paper to shreds in Frankie's pocket.

"Why are you still here, Henry?" Mr Love asked.

"I'm just, uh, super interested in photography. Thought I'd watch how it's done," I said.

I don't mean to be vain, but that was perhaps the best possible thing I could have said at that moment because, one, I created a believable excuse for hanging around. Two, I made Mr Love think I was interested in something sort of school-related and, three, I formed an unspoken allegiance with the photographer, based on our shared love of photography.

"Well, Henry," Mr Love said, still trying to force the sword out of its sheath. "A knighted king needs a squire. Get my crown from that table there, and then you can help me with my armaments."

FLASH. The photographer took a picture.

"Hey!" Mr Love shouted. "I wasn't ready."

"But I was. I'm only paid till three, you know."

"I'll pay you overtime, for as long as it takes."

"I think it could take a while," the photographer said. "Have you considered that the photo might look better with the visor down?"

"No," Mr Love barked. He gave his sword

a final yank. It came free with such force that it sent him spiralling into the chair, knocking it over. He fell on his bum — the only place not armoured. "I need a hand here, Henry! And where's my crown?"

"I was so close." I sighed, and moped over to pick up Mr Love's crown. Then, from down the hall, came the echoing sound of two people yelling.

"Shouldn't you check that out?" I hollered to Mr Love.

But Mr Love was in no position to help. He had become a metallic human pretzel. He would impale himself on his own sword if he wasn't careful.

I crept down the hall to the room where the yelling was coming from. There was a glass window in the door and I peeked through it. What I saw made me immediately duck down again, out of view.

Mum and Dad were in there. Both of them were standing up, arguing nose to nose, their chairs overturned. Emily was still seated, but she'd made herself about as small as a ferret. At the other end of the room, a smartly dressed woman was rapidly taking notes.

"Hey, Zipzer man! You made it back. What are you doing on the floor?"

I turned and saw Frankie and Ashley jogging up to me. I sidled along the wall, doing my best spider impression, until I was out of view of the window.

"You actually did it," Frankie said, inspecting my new uniform. "And with three minutes to spare. Did you get the photo taken?"

"Nope, Mr Love – or should I say, Prince John – over there stole my thunder." I had failed in my mission.

"What's going on in there?" Ashley motioned to the window.

"Oh, nothing," I said. "Just my parents ruining Emily's life."

Frankie looked through the little window. "Why is your dad shirtless?"

"Who cares?" I said, and headed away from all the misery. "Let's get out of here and go play video games or something."

Ashley couldn't help sneaking a peek in through the window before we left. "Gross!"

"I was so close." I sighed.

"There's always next year." Frankie shrugged.

"Or," Ashley said, "I could use my computer to edit out all the purple once you get the picture."

"You'd probably have to edit out my entire face," I said. "Or..." I stopped talking because I'd seen something tempting – so very tempting.

The fire alarm!

"Or," I went on, my smile so big my lips extended beyond my face, "we could empty the school, and I could get it right this year."

I brushed my fingers over that oh-so-tempting button. What could be easier? All it would take was the slightest push.

"I've always wondered what happens when you push one of these things," I said.

"Me too," Ashley said, surprisingly.

"What do you guys think happens?" Frankie said. "The fire alarm goes off."

"Do it," Ashley whispered to me.

My finger hovered over the button, then I felt Ashley's hand press it down. She giggled, and a fraction of a second later, the school exploded with a siren so loud you'd think Martians were invading!

We scurried away. As we passed the open door to the school hall, I caught sight of Mr Love. He threw down his visor. "That is very inconvenient!" he yelled. "Follow me to the playground! Everyone to the playground!"

He clanked and clinked down the hall, the photographer trailing after him. "I'm still on the clock," he said to Mr Love. "Do you want me to take that sword?"

"A king never hands over his sword," Mr Love said, then louder, "Come on, pupils. Everyone, outside."

Every doorway in the school opened at once, and a stream of kids and teachers poured into the halls. We hung back, hiding behind some lockers before ducking into the lost property office. For a split second, I saw my dad through the crowds, and, yes, he was still shirtless.

Once everyone had left, we sneaked back to the school hall. I sat down on the metal chair and tried to act like there wasn't an ear-splitting alarm going off.

Ashley got behind the camera.

"Why do you get to take it?" Frankie screamed at her. He had to shout because the alarm was so loud.

"Because I know what I'm doing. Dad's been teaching me how to do x-rays."

"Hank hasn't broken any bones!" Frankie shouted.

"Somebody just take the photo before we're caught," I yelled.

Ashley put her eye to the viewfinder. "Gimme a smile. You can do better than that. Come on, work it, baby! Fierce eyes!"

Frankie and I exchanged blank looks.

Ashley sighed. "How about you just say cheese?"

"Cheese!" I cried, and flashed a perfect, million-dollar smile.

FLASH!

I rushed over to the camera to check out my likeness, and with my adrenaline pumping, I sort of shouldered Ashley out of the way.

"Hey!" she cried.

"Relax, man," Frankie said. "She got the shot."

"I have to delete my bad one," I said. I scrolled through hundreds of pictures in a folder marked "Westbrook Academy photos". For some reason, my pushing finger got tired at precisely the moment that Miss Adolf's photo popped onto the screen. She was smiling. Gross!

"Get it away!" Frankie cried.

"OK, OK." I scrolled faster and faster, until I got to the photo that I hoped no one would ever see, not Frankie, not Ashley, not my family, and certainly no one in the future. Especially those people who were deciding which kid should be the first in space.

I won't even *describe* it to you. It was worse than I'd imagined. Much worse. It was like every weird face I'd ever made in my entire life compressed into one image. Plus, it was out of focus. Plus, I had moved when it was taken, so I looked like I was about to eat my own eyeballs. Plus, I was drenched in purple slime. Plus— Forget it, I've said enough.

"And you are outta here, buddy," I said and pushed the "Delete" button.

But I wasn't finished. A menu came up on the camera. It said something weird about "dillute fielder," and a bunch of wiggly numbers started flashing. I just pushed the button with the only letter that wasn't dancing all over the place: Y.

"Noooo!!!" Ashley cried.

"What?"

"Congrats, Hank," Frankie said. "You just deleted the folder."

"Right," I said, "the folder with my bad photo."

"And everyone else's OK-to-excellent photos," Ashley said.

"Where's the undelete button?" I asked. There was no answer. "Guys, where's the undelete button?"

"There is no undelete button," Ashley said.

"There must be!"

Now my heart was really racing as I pushed the "N" button, and then I pushed every other button on the stupid camera.

"Dude," Frankie said. "Let it go."

"Never."

"No, really, you have to let it go."

"Why?" I asked, not looking up.

"Because—" Frankie said.

I felt a hand grab my shoulder and squeeze.

"Relax, buddy," I said without thinking. "Where's the fire?"

"You tell me, young man."

I spun around and found myself looking up at a fireman, wearing breathing apparatus and holding an axe. I flashed him my million-dollar smile. He wasn't impressed.

Oh, boy.

CHAPTER TWENTY

We all got the punishments we deserved. Me, Frankie and Ashley had detention for a week, and we each had to write a five-paragraph essay on fire safety. Actually, Miss Adolf made *mine* ten paragraphs, because she's Miss Adolf.

Also — and this wasn't part of my official punishment, but it sure felt like it — I'd had a long-standing appointment with my dentist for the day after the photo shoot. He found two cavities and extracted one baby molar that was refusing to fall out on its own, and it was absolute torture.

Emily and Dad had to make Mum breakfast for two weeks, and Dad also had to give her a hand massage every evening. Plus, Dad had to buy new clothes, more appropriately fitting ones, all picked out by Mum. And she threw out his lucky jumper.

With all the tension from the disastrous interview with the institute, I didn't catch any flack at home. Mum and Dad hadn't been told that *I* was sort of the one who set off the fire alarm. And steadfast Katherine the lizard kept her lizard mouth shut. She never once mentioned that I had poured liquid soap all over Emily's dentist-recommended hypersonic toothbrush.

Actually, I was doing pretty well with my parents. My school photo came a week ago and it wasn't bad at all. It was pretty good. It wasn't amazing, but it looked like what I normally see in the mirror. Not weird, not perfection, just ... me. And that was OK.

I thought I'd proved to my family that I could do something right in school, even if that something right only lasted for a fraction of a second. Even if it did take three uniforms and a fire alarm to achieve it.

I stared at the photo in admiration as Mum put it on the shelf. "Looking smart, Hank," she said, plopping down next to me on the sofa. "How's it coming in there?" she shouted through to the kitchen. "I'm starving!"

Dad and Emily were sweating over the open flame, shirtsleeves rolled up, bickering between themselves. Just then the post slipped through the letterbox.

Emily abandoned Mum's eggs and dashed for the door. She tore through the stack of mail, tossing aside everything until her fingers landed on a big manila envelope. She ripped it open with her teeth.

"It's from the institute!" she cried.

"Now, Em," Mum said, "there's always

next year, sweetie. So don't take it too—"

"I got in!" Emily screamed.

"What?" Mum sat up. "How?"

"Let's see," Emily said. "Here, it begins, 'Dear, Emily, We are delighted to offer you a spot... You were one of the strongest candidates we interviewed all year.' And there's more about how I should feel proud of myself and expect to win Nobel prizes in twenty years, and here's the best bit — 'Out of all the candidates, we feel you would benefit the most from spending time in a less chaotic and more nurturing environment.'"

"Charming," Mum said with a frown.

"That's what it says, Mum. Should I read it again?"

"No," Mum said, picking up the rest of the post. She sorted through it. "Here's a letter from school. Oh, it's from Mr Love... Hmm."

"He's an odd one," said my dad from the

kitchen, "although I did like his sword."

"You can tell him in person," Mum said. "He wants us to come in. He wants to talk about the missing photos. What missing photos? Hank! HANK!"

But I had already bolted. I was out of the door and running straight for the surface of Mars.